From Andrew, Valerie, Katie [...]
Christmas 2003

FIVE
FAVOURITE
FAIRY
TALES

All Ladybird books are available at most bookshops,
supermarkets and newsagents, or can be ordered direct from:
Ladybird Postal Sales
PO Box 133 Paignton TQ3 2YP England
Telephone: (+44) 01803 554761
Fax: (+44) 01803 663394

A catalogue record for this book is available
from the British Library

Published by Ladybird Books Ltd
A subsidiary of the Penguin Group
A Pearson Company
© LADYBIRD BOOKS LTD MCMXCVIII
Stories in this book were previously published by Ladybird Books Ltd
in the *Favourite Tales* series.

LADYBIRD and the device of a Ladybird are trademarks of
Ladybird Books Ltd Loughborough Leicestershire UK

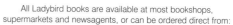

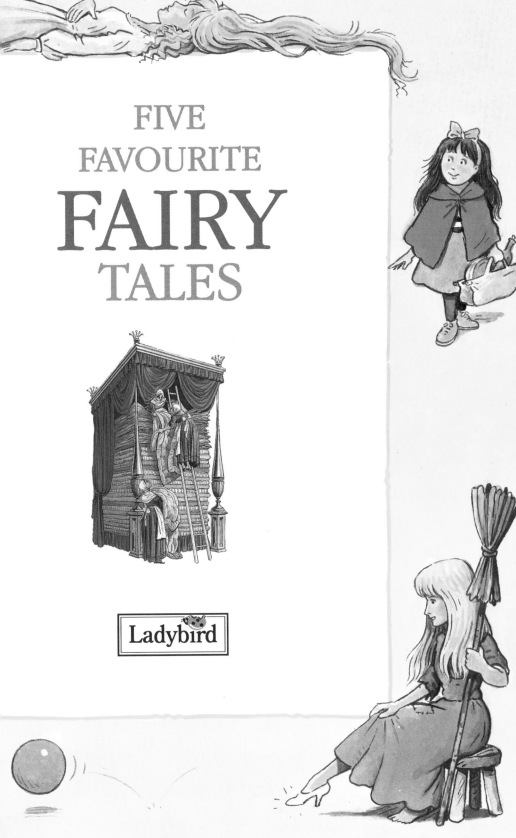

FIVE
FAVOURITE
FAIRY
TALES

Ladybird

Introduction

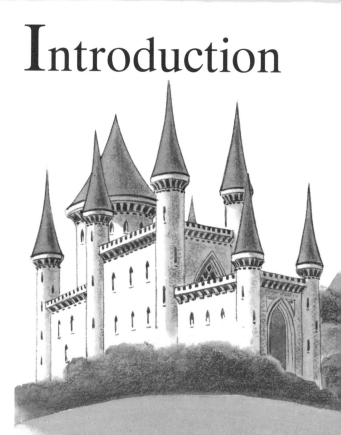

Children will treasure this collection of timeless fairy tales. The easy-to-read retellings, enhanced by exciting, richly colourful illustrations, faithfully capture all the magic of the original stories.

Contents

Cinderella

Sleeping Beauty

Little Red Riding Hood

Rapunzel

Based on the story by
Jacob and Wilhelm Grimm

Illustrated by Martin Aitchison

The Princess and the Pea

Based on the story by
Hans Christian Andersen

Illustrated by Robert Ayton

Stories retold by Nicola Baxter

Cover and Borders illustrated by
Peter Stevenson

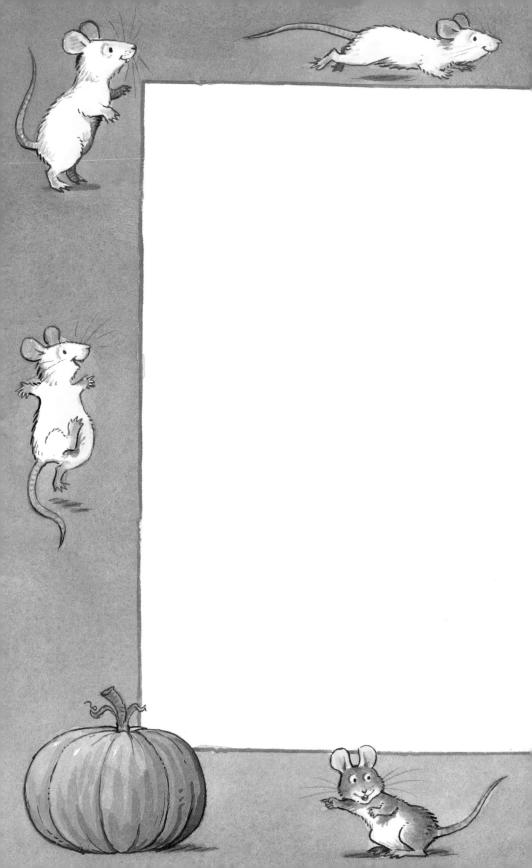

Cinderella

Once upon a time there was a young girl called Cinderella.

She lived with her father and two stepsisters. While her stepsisters spent their time buying pretty new clothes and going to parties, Cinderella wore old, ragged clothes and had to do all the hard work in the house.

The two sisters were selfish, unkind girls, which showed in their faces. Even wearing their fine clothes, they never looked as sweet and pretty as Cinderella.

One day a royal messenger came to announce that there was to be a grand ball at the King's palace.

The ball was in honour of the Prince, the King's only son.

Cinderella's sisters were both excited.
The Prince was very handsome, and
he had not yet found a bride.

When the evening of the ball arrived,
Cinderella had to help her sisters get
ready.

"Fetch my gloves!" cried one sister.

"Where are my jewels?" shrieked the
other.

They didn't think for a minute that
Cinderella might like to go to the ball!

When her sisters had driven
off in their fine carriage,
Cinderella sat all by
herself and cried
bitterly.

"Why are you crying, my dear?" said a voice. Cinderella looked up and was amazed to see her fairy godmother smiling down at her.

"I wish *I* could go to the ball and meet the Prince," Cinderella said, wiping away her tears.

"Then you shall!" laughed her fairy godmother. "But you must do exactly as I say."

"Oh, I *will*," promised Cinderella.

"Then go into the garden and fetch the biggest pumpkin you can find," said the fairy.

So Cinderella found an enormous pumpkin and brought it to her fairy godmother. With a wave of her magic wand, the fairy changed the pumpkin into a wonderful golden coach.

"Now bring me six white mice from the kitchen," the godmother said. Cinderella did as she was told.

Waving her wand again, the fairy godmother changed the mice into six gleaming white horses to pull the coach! Cinderella rubbed her eyes in amazement.

Then Cinderella looked down at her old ragged clothes. "Oh dear!" she sighed. "How can I go to the ball in this old dress?"

For the third time, her godmother waved her magic wand. In a trice, Cinderella was wearing a lovely white ballgown trimmed with blue silk ribbons. There were jewels in her hair, and on her feet were dainty glass dancing slippers.

"Now off you go!" said her fairy godmother, smiling. "Just remember one thing – the magic only lasts until midnight!"

So Cinderella went off to the ball in her sparkling golden coach.

In the royal palace, everyone was enchanted by the beautiful girl in the white and blue dress. "Who *is* she?" they whispered.

The Prince thought Cinderella was the loveliest girl he had ever seen.

"May I have the honour of this dance?" he asked, bowing low.

All the other girls were jealous of the mysterious stranger.

Cinderella danced with the Prince all evening. She forgot her fairy godmother's warning until... *dong... dong... dong...* the clock began to strike midnight... *dong... dong... dong...*

Cinderella ran from the ballroom without a word... *dong... dong... dong...*

In her hurry, she lost one of her glass slippers... *dong... dong... dong.* The Prince ran out just as the lovely girl slipped out of sight.

"I don't even know her name," he sighed.

When Cinderella's sisters arrived home from the ball, they could talk of nothing but the beautiful girl who had danced with the Prince all evening.

"You can't imagine how annoying it was!" they cried. "After the wretched girl left in such a hurry, he wouldn't dance at all!"

Cinderella hardly heard their complaining. Her head and her heart were whirling with memories of the handsome Prince who had held her in his arms.

Meanwhile, the Prince was determined to find the mysterious beauty who had stolen his heart. The glass slipper was the only clue he had.

"The girl whose foot will fit this slipper shall be my wife," he said.

So the Prince set out to search the kingdom for his bride. A royal messenger carried the slipper on a silk cushion.

Every girl in the land wanted to try on the slipper. But although many tried, the slipper was always too small and too dainty.

At last the Prince came to Cinderella's house.

Each ugly sister in turn tried to squeeze her foot into the elegant slipper, but it was no use. Their feet were far too big and clumsy.

"Do you have any other daughters?" the Prince asked Cinderella's father.

"One more," he replied.

"Oh no," cried the sisters. "She is much too busy in the kitchen!" But the Prince insisted that *all* the sisters must try the slipper.

Cinderella hung her head in shame. She did not want the Prince to see her in her old clothes. But she sat down and tried on the dainty slipper. Of course, it fitted her perfectly!

The Prince looked at Cinderella's sweet face and recognised the girl he had danced with. "It *is* you," he whispered. "Please be my bride, and we shall never be parted again."

How happy Cinderella was! Her fairy godmother appeared and, waving her magic wand, dressed Cinderella in a gown fit for a princess.

Then the Prince led Cinderella home to the royal palace.

Cinderella and her Prince were married at the most magnificent wedding that anyone could remember. Kings and queens from many lands came to meet the new Princess and wish her well.

Even Cinderella's sisters had to agree that she was the loveliest bride they had ever seen.

And Cinderella and her Prince lived
happily ever after.

Sleeping
Beauty

Once upon a time there was a king and a queen who had long hoped for a child of their own. When, at last, a baby princess was born, they thought that a good fairy must have been looking after them.

"I shall invite all the fairies in the kingdom to come to our baby's christening!" cried the King joyfully.

When the time for the christening
came, the King was as good as his word.

Among the guests were the twelve
good fairies who lived in that land.
After the grand feast, each of them
gave a magic gift to the baby girl.

"You shall have a lovely face," said
the first.

"You shall be gentle and loving," said
another.

One by one, they promised the little
Princess all the good things in the
world.

When eleven of the fairies had given their gifts, a furious voice was heard at the doorway.

"I suppose you thought I was too old
to do magic now! Well, I'll show you!"
it shrieked. And a very old fairy,
whom everyone had forgotten, walked
slowly towards the cradle.

"When the Princess is fifteen years
old, she shall prick her finger on a
spindle and fall down dead," she
cursed, and rushed from the palace.

The King was horrified. "Oh, how can I have forgotten her?" he cried. "And what shall we do now?"

"I may be able to help," said a gentle voice.

It was the twelfth fairy. "I can't undo the evil spell," she said, "but I can soften it a little. The Princess will prick her finger on a spindle, but she will not die. She will just fall asleep for a hundred years."

The King and Queen were very grateful to the twelfth fairy, but still they did not want anything to happen to their precious daughter. They made sure that all the spindles in the kingdom were destroyed.

Year by year, the Princess grew more
lovely. Surely no one could want to
harm such a kind and gentle girl?

On the morning of her fifteenth birthday, as the Princess wandered through the palace, she climbed to a high tower where she had never been before. There she saw a wooden door.

Pushing it open gently, she peeped inside. There sat an old, old woman at a spinning wheel.

"Good morning," said the Princess. "What are you doing?"

"I am spinning, my child," said the old woman. "Look!" and she handed the Princess the sharp spindle. At that moment, the Princess pricked her delicate finger!

At once, the Princess fell into a deep, deep sleep. The wicked fairy's words had come true.

At the same moment, everyone in the palace fell asleep as well.

n the great hall, the King and Queen
ell asleep on their golden thrones.

The lords and ladies, the palace
guards, and all the servants fell into a
deep slumber. The whole palace was
silent and still.

As the years passed, a hedge of thorns and brambles grew up around the palace walls. It grew so tall and so thick that at last only the flags above the highest towers could be seen.

The story of the beautiful sleeping Princess spread through the kingdom and far beyond.

She became known as the Sleeping Beauty.

Many princes came to the palace, hoping to rescue the Princess, but none could force his way through the thick, sharp thorns.

Almost a hundred years had passed since the Princess had pricked her finger, when a handsome young Prince from a faraway kingdom happened to pass by.

On the road he met an old man, who remembered a story that his grandfather had told him. And so it was that the Prince heard the legend of the Sleeping Beauty.

"I shall not rest until I have seen her and woken her," he vowed.

When the Prince saw the great hedge
of thorns, he nearly despaired. But
when he raised his sword, the thorns
suddenly turned into lovely roses, and
the hedge opened to let him through.

Inside the palace gates, all was still.
The dogs lay asleep in the courtyard.
The guards slept at their posts. Even
the pigeons sat asleep on the
rooftops. Not a sound could be heard.

The Prince searched the entire castle. He found the sleeping King and Queen and their sleeping servants. But it was not until he reached the very last room in the highest tower that he found Sleeping Beauty herself.

He gazed at her lovely face in wonder. "I would give my whole kingdom if you would wake and be my bride," he whispered.

Then he bent over and gently kissed
the sleeping girl.

At the touch of the Prince's lips, Sleeping Beauty awoke. As she smiled at him, she felt as if she had loved him all her life.

Throughout the palace there were sounds of laughter. Everyone woke and rubbed their eyes. They could hardly believe that the evil spell had been lifted at last.

As for Sleeping Beauty and her Prince, they were married soon after. And the King made sure that *everyone* was invited to the wedding!

Little Red Riding Hood

Once upon a time there was a little girl who loved to visit her grandmother. The old woman was always busy making something for her favourite granddaughter.

One day she made something very special indeed. It was a beautiful, bright red cape with a hood. The little girl loved it so much that she wore it all the time!

Soon everyone started calling her "Little Red Riding Hood".

One morning the little girl's mother said, "Little Red Riding Hood, your grandmother is not very well. I am packing up some things to help her feel better and I'd like you to take them to her.

"But *do* be careful as you walk through the forest. And *don't* stop for anything on the way!"

"I'll be *very* careful," promised Little
Red Riding Hood, "and I won't stop
for a second."

So off she went with her little basket.
She waved to her mother until she
was out of sight.

Just at the edge of the forest, a very crafty fellow was waiting.

It was a wolf! When Little Red Riding Hood passed by, he greeted her with a slow smile.

"Good morning, my dear," he said. "And what a fine morning it is!"

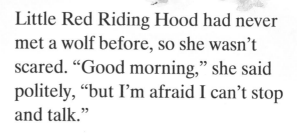

Little Red Riding Hood had never met a wolf before, so she wasn't scared. "Good morning," she said politely, "but I'm afraid I can't stop and talk."

"No matter, my dear," said the wolf. "I shall walk along with you. Where are you off to, this fine morning?"

"I'm going to see my grandmother," replied Little Red Riding Hood.

"Then I think I can be of service," said the wolf. "I'll show you where there are some lovely flowers, my dear. You can take her a bouquet."

Little Red Riding Hood knew that she shouldn't stop, but she did like the idea of taking her grandmother a special present. So she followed the wolf.

"Here we are," he said. "Now I must fly. I am late for my lunch."

 When Little Red Riding Hood reached her grandmother's house, she was a little bit surprised to see that the door was open.

"Is that you, my dear?" croaked a faint voice. "Do come in!"

But when Little Red Riding Hood crept up to her grandmother's bed, a very strange sight met her eyes.

"Oh, Grandmother!" she cried. "What big ears you have!"

"All the better to hear you with, my dear," came the reply.

Little Red Riding Hood went a little closer.

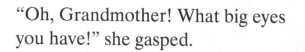

"Oh, Grandmother! What big eyes you have!" she gasped.

"All the better to see you with, my dear!"

Little Red Riding Hood took one more step.

"Oh, Grandmother! What big teeth you have!"

"All the better to eat you with!" cried the wolf, and he gobbled her up!

When Little Red Riding Hood did not come home that afternoon, her parents were very worried. At last her father went to Grandmother's cottage to find her.

How horrified he was when he found a fierce animal in Grandmother's bed! With one blow of his axe, he killed the wicked wolf.

Then Little Red Riding Hood's father carefully cut open the wolf. Out jumped the little girl! She felt very strange indeed.

"Where is Grandmother?" she asked.

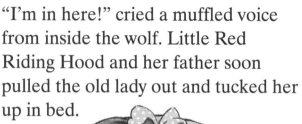

"I'm in here!" cried a muffled voice from inside the wolf. Little Red Riding Hood and her father soon pulled the old lady out and tucked her up in bed.

"I feel a lot better now!" said Little Red Riding Hood's grandmother, as she tasted the good things the little girl had brought.

Little Red Riding Hood's mother was so glad her little girl was safe that she hadn't the heart to scold her.

"I know you won't stop to pick flowers next time, Little Red Riding Hood," she said, "because *I* will give you some to take to Grandmother!"

Rapunzel

Once upon a time, in a faraway land, there lived a man and his wife. They had a pretty little house and all that they needed, but one thing made them unhappy.

"If only we had a child of our own to love and look after," they sighed.

Next to their house stood an old
mansion with a beautiful garden.
People said that a wicked witch lived
there. One day, the wife glimpsed
some lettuces growing in the
next-door garden.

Although she went on with her work, the lettuces stayed in her mind. Finally, she said to her husband, "I feel I shall die if I don't taste one of those crisp, green lettuces. Won't you please climb over the wall and get one for me?"

Her husband was afraid to go into the garden, so at first he refused. But as the days passed, the wife's yearning for the lettuces grew, until at last she became quite ill.

One night, the man could bear it no longer, and he climbed over the wall. As his feet touched the ground, he nearly fainted with fright. There before him stood the witch.

"How dare you come creeping into my garden?" she snarled.

"I must have some lettuces for my wife," the man pleaded. "She is ill, and she will die without them."

"Take the lettuces, then," said the witch. "But in return, you must give your firstborn child to me."

The man was so terrified that he agreed. Grabbing a handful of lettuces, he fled back to his wife.

Some time later, a beautiful baby girl was born to the man and his wife. That same day, the witch appeared at their door. Reminding the man of his promise, she took the baby away.

The witch named the child Rapunzel,
and she looked after her well. Every
year the girl grew more lovely.

So that no one should ever see how beautiful she was, the witch shut Rapunzel up in a high tower in the forest. The tower had no door and no staircase – just one window right at the top.

Only the witch ever visited poor Rapunzel. She would call out,

"Rapunzel, Rapunzel,
Let down your hair."

Rapunzel's hair shone like gold in the sun, and it was so long that it reached from the top of the tower right down to the ground.

Huffing and puffing, the wicked witch would slowly climb the tower, holding on to Rapunzel's lovely hair. Then she would climb in through the window.

Years passed, and Rapunzel never set
eyes on another living person. Then,
one day, a young prince riding
through the forest heard Rapunzel's
sweet singing.

"I have never heard such a lovely voice," he said to himself. "I shall not rest until I find out who it belongs to."

So the Prince hid nearby and saw the witch climb the tower.

That evening, after the witch had gone, the Prince called out,

"Rapunzel, Rapunzel,
Let down your hair."

Rapunzel was astonished to see a young man climb through the window. And the Prince was dazzled by the lovely girl. As they spoke to each other, they realised they were in love.

"I will come back tomorrow night to rescue you," the Prince promised.

When the witch returned the next day, she saw at once that Rapunzel's heart was full of love for a stranger.

"You have betrayed me, you wicked girl!" she shrieked furiously. With her sharp scissors, she went *snipper snap!* and cut off Rapunzel's hair. Then she took the girl to a distant desert and left her there, alone and weeping.

The witch returned to the tower to wait for the Prince. At last she heard him call,

"Rapunzel, Rapunzel,
Let down your hair,"

and she lowered the golden plait for him to climb.

When the Prince found himself face to face with the angry witch, he leapt in despair from the tower. He fell into a thicket of briars, which scratched his eyes and blinded him.

For years the Prince wandered
through many lands, until one day,
in a lonely desert, he heard the lovely
voice that he had never forgotten.

"Rapunzel!" he cried, throwing his arms around her. Rapunzel's tears of joy fell on the Prince's eyes and healed them. Once more he saw her beautiful face.

The Prince took Rapunzel's hand and
led her to his kingdom, where they
were married with great rejoicing.

And there, safe at last from the wicked witch, Rapunzel and her Prince lived happily ever after.

The Princess
and the Pea

Once upon a time, in a kingdom far away, there lived a handsome young prince. The time had come for him to find a princess to marry.

"She must be a *real* princess," the Prince told the King and Queen. "That is the most important thing of all."

So the Prince rode off to search for
a real princess.

He travelled far and wide for many
years. Whenever he saw a castle, he
stopped to find out if a real princess
lived there.

On his travels, the Prince met many clever and beautiful ladies, but he was never quite sure if they were *real* princesses. For a real princess is a very special person, and there are very few of them to be found.

At last, sad and lonely, the Prince returned home.

One night a terrible storm raged around the castle where the Prince lived with the King and Queen. Rain beat against the old stone walls, and thunder roared overhead.

As lightning flashed across the sky, a small figure struggled through the rain and knocked on the castle door.

Inside, all the servants were hiding, frightened of the storm. The King himself went to see who was knocking on such a wild night.

The King was astonished to see a beautiful young girl standing outside! She was shivering with cold, and dripping from head to foot.

"My dear, come in at once!" cried the King. He led the lovely stranger to the warm room where the Queen and the Prince were waiting.

As soon as he saw her, the Prince fell in love with the beautiful girl.

He was filled with happiness when she curtsied and said, "Your Majesties, I am a *real* Princess."

"Well, well," thought the Queen, "we'll soon find out whether she's a *real* princess." While the lovely visitor put on dry clothes, the Queen herself went to see that a comfortable bed was made ready.

Right at the bottom of the bed, on the very first mattress, the Queen put a tiny green pea. Then she said, "Bring more mattresses! Hurry!"

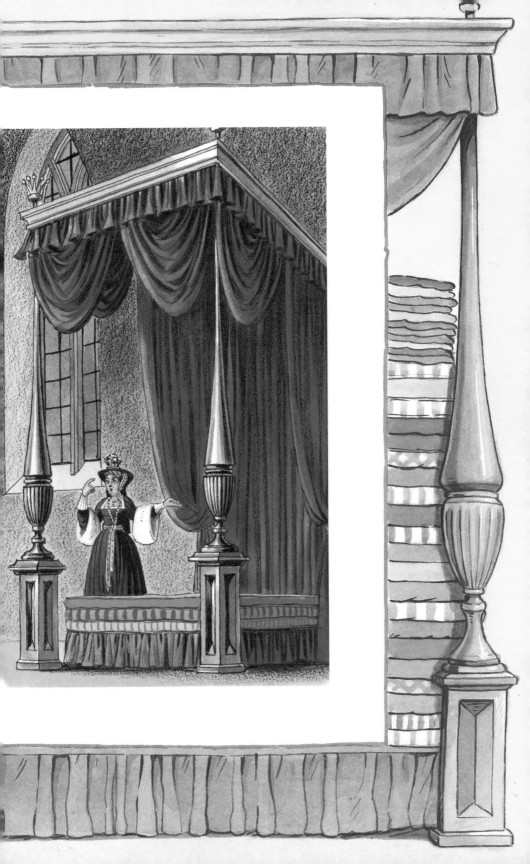

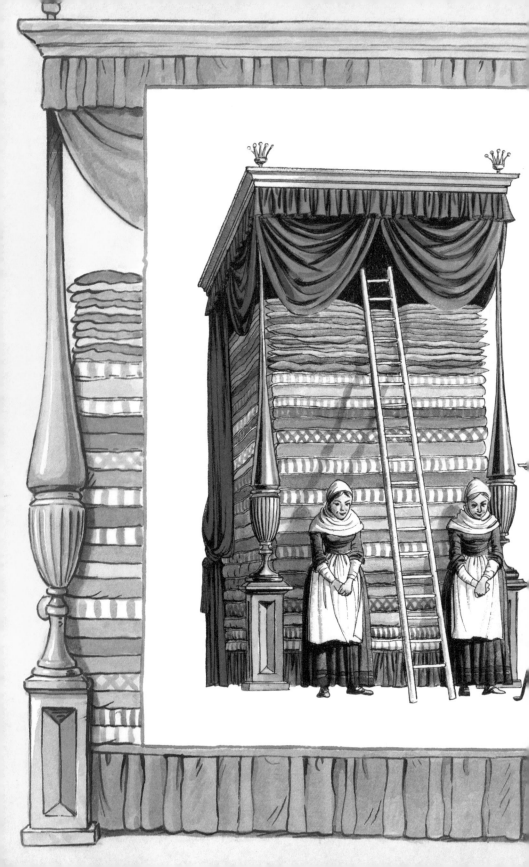

At last the bed was ready. There were so many mattresses that a ladder was needed to reach the top!

"I hope you will have a comfortable night, my dear," said the Queen, leading her visitor to bed.

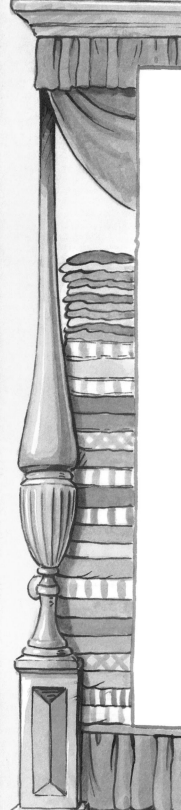

In the morning, the Queen hurried to find out if her plan had worked.

The young girl was already awake and sitting up in bed.

"Did you sleep well, my dear?" asked the Queen.

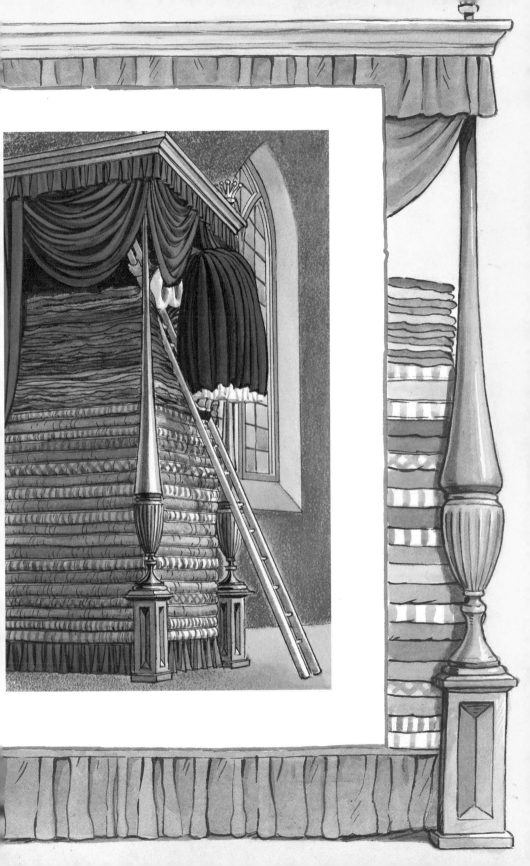

"I'm afraid I didn't sleep at all," the girl replied. "There was something hard in the bed, and it has made me black and blue all over."

The Queen smiled. "Only a *real* princess would have such delicate skin that she could feel a pea through so many mattresses," she said.

When the Queen told the Prince the news, he was overjoyed. "At last I have found you!" he told the Princess. "Please say you will be my bride."

The Princess shone with happiness. "I will," she whispered.

So the Prince and the Princess were married, amid great rejoicing.

As for the pea, it was put in a
museum. People came from far
and near to look at it.

"You see," they said to each other,
"our princess is a *real* princess. She
is a very special person indeed!"